Florence
the Friendship
Fairy

Special thanks to Sue Mongredien

For Hannah Powell, who gave
me the idea for Florence in
the first place. Thank you!

ISBN 978-0-545-45572-5

All rights reserved. Published by Scholastic Inc., 557 Broadway, New
York, NY 10012, by arrangement with Rainbow Magic Limited.

12 11 10 9 8 7 6 5 4   14 15 16 17/0

Printed in the U.S.A.   40

First Scholastic printing, December 2012

Florence
the Friendship
Fairy

by Daisy Meadows

SCHOLASTIC INC.

The Fairyland Palace

Maypole

Bandstand

Stalls

Treasure Hunt

Kirsty's House

Wetherbury Village

The fairies are planning a Friendship Day
But I'll soon take their smiles away.
I'll ruin it all, I'll wreck their fun,
I'll break up the friendships one by one!

I'll steal Florence's magic things
And laugh at the misery that this act brings!
A ribbon, a book, some bracelets, too —
She really won't know what to do.

Friendship will be finished, wait and see.
Soon everyone will be friendless, just like me!

**Find the hidden letters in the stars
throughout this book. Unscramble all 10 letters
to spell two special friendship words!**

Contents

Magic Memories   1

Friendship and Frost!   9

On the Goblin Trail   17

Boo!   27

A Tempting Offer   37

Magic Memories

Rachel Walker pulled a large scrapbook from underneath Kirsty Tate's bed, and the two best friends opened it between them. It was their memory book, full of souvenirs from all the exciting times they'd shared together.

"That vacation on Rainspell Island was really special," Rachel said, pointing

at the ferry tickets and map that had
been stuck into the book.

"I know," Kirsty replied, smiling. "It
was the first time we met each other —
and the first time we met the fairies,
too!" She lowered her voice. "I wonder if
we'll have a fairy adventure this week."

"I hope so," Rachel said, feeling her
heart thump excitedly at the thought.
She and her parents were spending her
school vacation with Kirsty's family, and
she had been wondering the same thing

herself. Somehow, extra-special things always seemed to happen when she and Kirsty got together!

The girls kept looking through their book. There was the museum pamphlet from the day they'd met Storm the Lightning Fairy; tickets to Strawberry Farms, where they'd helped Georgia the Guinea Pig Fairy; plus all sorts of photos, postcards, maps, petals, and leaves. . . .

Kirsty frowned when she spotted an empty space on one page. "Did a picture fall out?" she wondered.

"It must have," Rachel said. "You can see that something was stuck there before. I think it was a picture of the fairy models we painted the day we met Willow the Wednesday Fairy. I wonder where it went."

As the girls turned more pages, they realized that photo wasn't the only thing missing. A map of the constellations that Kirsty's gran had given them the night they'd helped Stephanie the Starfish Fairy had vanished, and so had the all-access pass they'd had for the Fairyland Games. Each time they turned a page, they discovered something even worse.

"Oh, no! This photo of us at Camp Stargaze is torn," Rachel said in dismay.

"This page has scribbles all over it," Kirsty cried. "How did that happen?"

"And where did *this* picture come from?" Rachel asked, pointing at a colorful image of a pretty little fairy. She had shoulder-length blond hair that was pinned back with a pink star-shaped clip. She wore a sparkly lilac top and a ruffled blue skirt with a colorful belt, and pink sparkly ankle boots. "I've never even seen her before!" She bit her lip. "Something weird is going on, Kirsty. You don't think —"

Before Rachel could finish her sentence, the picture of the fairy began to sparkle and glitter with all the colors of the rainbow. The girls watched, wide-eyed,

as the fairy fluttered her wings, stretched, and then flew right off the page in a whirl of twinkling dust!

"Oh!" Kirsty gasped. "Hello! What's your name? How did you get into our memory book?"

The fairy smiled, shook out her wings, and flew a loop-the-loop. "I'm Florence the Friendship Fairy," she said in a sweet voice, her bright eyes darting around the room. "You're Kirsty and Rachel, aren't you? I've heard so much about you! I know you've been good friends to the fairies many, many times before."

"It's so nice to meet you," Rachel said. "But, Florence, do you know what happened to our memory book? Things are missing from the pages, and some things have even been ruined."

Florence fluttered over and landed on the bed. "I'm afraid that's the reason I came here," she said sadly. "Special memory books, scrapbooks, and photo albums everywhere have been ruined and stolen — so I need your help!"

Friendship and Frost!

The girls were confused, so Florence explained. "As the friendship fairy, I do my best to keep friendships strong throughout the human world and the fairy world, too," she said. "Like you, I have a memory book that I fill with my nicest friendship memories — party invitations, pressed flowers, pictures . . ."

"That sounds beautiful," Rachel said with a smile.

"It is," Florence replied. "Best of all, it's full of special friendship magic. When my book is with me, its magic protects all the special friendship mementos made and collected by friends all over the world. It also keeps the wonderful memories inside them safe! But unfortunately . . ."

"Don't tell me — Jack Frost has done something horrible again!" Kirsty said knowingly. Jack Frost was a cruel, angry creature who was always doing awful things with the help of his sneaky goblins.

"Yes," said Florence glumly. "Jack Frost doesn't believe in friendship." She frowned. "I think he's jealous of other people having best friends and doing fun things together, because he doesn't have any friends. Everyone is too scared of him."

Rachel and Kirsty nodded. They had met Jack Frost many times before, and he was scary. He was always so mean and grumpy — and he had very strong magical powers, too.

"We fairies have been planning a special Friendship Day for tomorrow,"

Florence told them. "The Party Fairies have been helping get everything ready — the music, the outfits, the party games, the food. Oh, it's going to be so much fun! But when I was in the party workshop, I put down my memory book for a minute so I could help Cherry the Cake Fairy with her icing. Before I knew what was happening, the goblins had burst in and stolen my book!"

"Oh, no!" cried Rachel. "That's awful."

"Is that why our memory book has been ruined, too?" Kirsty asked.

"Yes," Florence said. "Since my memory

book was taken, other people's books and photo albums haven't been magically protected. I'm sure the goblins have taken the chance to go around ruining as many of them as they can!"

"Well, we'll help you find your magic book," Rachel said, her eyes gleaming with excitement at the thought of another fairy adventure. "Where do you think we should start looking?"

"Oh, thank you!" Florence said. "True friends always help one another." She fluttered over to perch on Kirsty's knee. "I've been following the goblins' trail. They're definitely in the human

world, and they've obviously been here in Wetherbury, since they messed up your book. So we could look around the village — do you think your parents will let you do that?"

"Yes," Kirsty replied. "Wetherbury is a small village, and I know most people here. Mom and Dad are fine with me being out, as long as I'm with a friend and I tell them where we're going. Maybe if we —" She broke off as she heard footsteps approaching. "Quick, Florence! Hide!" she whispered urgently.

On the Goblin Trail

With a whirl of sparkly fairy dust, Florence fluttered her wings and flew back into the book. She became a picture on the page once again.

Rachel smiled. Fairy magic was so amazing!

Kirsty's mom came into the room, holding her purse and a shopping bag.

"Girls, I'm just about to do some baking for the village-hall party, but I need a  couple things from the store. Would you mind —"

"We'll get them," Kirsty interrupted at once, flashing a grin at Rachel. "What do you need?" Kirsty's mom wrote a list and opened her purse. The party she'd mentioned was being held two days later, to celebrate the reopening of the village hall. Everyone in the village had helped restore the hall to its former glory and was planning to go to the party. It sounded like it was going to be a lot of fun.

While Mrs. Tate was looking in her

purse, Florence gave Rachel a wink. She flew out of the memory book in a flurry of pink sparkles and fluttered to hide in Rachel's pocket. Kirsty's mom looked up just as the last sparkle of magic dust disappeared — *phew!* — and gave Kirsty some money.

The girls headed out, with Florence peeking out of Rachel's pocket. They hadn't gone very far when they spotted a colorful scrap of paper blowing across the ground. Rachel pounced on it immediately. "Look, Kirsty, it's the ticket

to the flower show where we met Ella
the Rose Fairy!" she said. "The goblins
must have dropped it."

"So we know they
went this way!"
Kirsty said excitedly,
putting the paper
carefully into her bag.
She looked down the
street, hoping to spot a
flash of goblin green. "Let's head for
High Street."

The girls walked down Twisty Lane
and passed the village hall. It was
already decorated with strings of flags
for the party, and looked brand-new
with its fresh coat of paint.

As she was admiring it, Kirsty
spotted something stuck in a bush near

the entrance to the village hall's parking lot. "It's a candy wrapper," she said, picking it up and showing Rachel the shiny red paper. "But not an ordinary one."

"I recognize that!" Florence said eagerly. "Strawberry Sparkles — they're made by Honey the Candy Fairy!"

Rachel smiled, remembering the adventure she and Kirsty had with Honey. It had definitely been one of their  yummiest fairy missions! "That wrapper is from our memory book, too. We're still on the goblins' trail!"

The girls kept walking and were just

passing the park when they heard the
sound of grumpy voices arguing.

"Stop smiling, you look awful," one
voice complained. "And you two, stop
pushing each other."

"He keeps jabbing me," another
voice moaned. "Cut it out!"

"Ouch!"

The girls and
Florence looked
at one another.
"Sounds like
goblins!" Florence
whispered excitedly.
"Let's take a closer look."

Kirsty and Rachel slipped into the park
and hid behind a big flowering bush.
They peeked through the leaves to see

five bickering goblins. They were all
jostling one another as they posed for a
photograph.

"Ready?" called a sixth goblin.
"Say . . . UGLY!"

"UGLY!" they cried, all leering
horribly at the camera.

"Perfect," said the goblin with the
camera. "So we have a photo, some dirt,

a thistle, a few weeds . . . Our memory book is really coming along."

"Our stuff is way better than that silly fairy's," scoffed one of the other goblins. "Flowers and fairy dust and all sorts of pink stuff? Yuck!"

"Come on, let's find some more things," the tallest goblin ordered. "Put what you've collected in your pockets,

and don't forget the yucky fairy book. Jack Frost said we weren't allowed to let it out of our sight."

The goblins marched out of the park, heading for High Street. One was carrying a book with a purple and gold cover. Florence stiffened when she saw it.

"There's my book!" she cried. "We have to get it back. Follow those goblins!"

Boo!

Kirsty and Rachel hung back until the goblins were a safe distance away, then followed them along Twisty Lane. The goblins all seemed like they were in very good moods. They kept stopping to take photographs of one another! But these photos weren't like ones in ordinary memory books or albums — instead, the goblins took pictures of the strangest things.

"Take one of me with this great big snail!" one goblin cried eagerly, picking  up a large snail and balancing it on his head. "It's so nice and slimy!"

"Take one of us having a fight," another goblin suggested, as he elbowed a skinny goblin with knobby knees.

"Hey, cut it out!" yelled the skinny goblin.

Click! Click! went the camera at the snail, the fight, and then a pile of garbage that another goblin found.

"Ahh, this is what good memories are all about," said the smallest goblin, who had mean, squinty eyes. "Hey, what about a photo of me ripping up this silly fairy book? That would be great!"

Florence gasped as he grabbed the memory book. It looked like he was going to tear it with his warty green fingers! "No!" she cried, zooming through the air before Kirsty or Rachel could stop her. "Don't do that!"

The goblins spun around at the sound of her little voice. "Oh, great," the tallest one moaned. "Just what we *didn't* want. A silly fairy, here to ruin everything. Quick, run!"

The goblins sprinted away. The small goblin was still holding Florence's precious memory book! As he ran, pretty flowers and sparkly treasures dropped from its pages. Florence looked like she wanted to cry!

"They're ruining it!" she wailed, swooping down and waving her magic wand to make all the items fairy-size. She collected everything that had fallen out of her memory book.

Meanwhile, the goblins were getting away. The girls didn't want to lose sight of them! "Florence, could you use your magic to turn us into fairies?" Kirsty asked, thinking fast. "That way we can fly after the goblins."

"Good idea," Florence said, pointing

her wand at the girls and whispering some magic words.

Instantly, a stream of bright sparkles flew out from her wand and swirled all around Kirsty and Rachel. Then they were shrinking smaller and smaller — and they had their own shining fairy wings on their backs. Even Kirsty's shopping bag had shrunk down to fairy-size!

Luckily, nobody was around to see them as the three fairies flew up into the air and began zooming after the goblins.

"We need a plan," Rachel said thoughtfully. In the distance, the goblins had reached a row of stores and had slowed down. They obviously thought they'd gotten away from the fairies.

"If we could somehow get that small goblin to drop the book . . ." Kirsty said, thinking aloud. "Maybe we can make him jump, and he might let go of it?"

"And then I could use my magic to shrink it back to fairy-size, and fly in to grab it!" Florence finished.

The three friends smiled at one another. "We could fly up behind the goblins so that we're really close to them," Rachel suggested. "Then Florence could turn us back into girls, and we could shout really loudly. That should make them jump!"

Kirsty giggled. "It would make *me* jump," she said. "Come on, let's try it."

Silently, the fairies flew as close to the goblins as they dared. Luckily, the goblins had their backs turned. They were busy peering into the candy shop, moaning that there weren't any bogmallows inside. When Kirsty and Rachel were hovering just behind the goblin holding Florence's memory book, Florence waved her wand and turned them back into girls.

"BOO!" Rachel and Kirsty shouted at the top of their lungs.

"Aarrrgh!" screamed the goblins, turning around in fear. But unfortunately, the smallest goblin didn't drop the book as they'd hoped. In fact, he only clutched it tighter — and all the goblins ran off down the street!

A Tempting Offer

"After them!" cried Florence, flying through the air like a streak of light. Kirsty and Rachel followed on foot, running as fast as they could.

The goblins ducked down an alley, with Florence and the girls right behind them. Kirsty grinned as she realized that the alley was a dead end. Soon, the goblins would be trapped!

Sure enough, the goblins realized there was nowhere else to run. They stopped and turned, their backs against the wall.

The smallest goblin hid the memory book behind him, a determined gleam in his eye. "You're not getting this back," he said rudely.

"I don't know why you want *my* memory book, anyway," Florence said. "You goblins hate pink sparkly things. Wouldn't you rather have a nice green memory book of your own?"

"Well, yes," the tallest goblin said, shrugging. "But we don't have one. So we're taking yours instead."

This gave Rachel an idea. "But if we could find you the perfect goblin memory book with a gorgeous green cover, would you . . . trade?" she asked, crossing her fingers behind her back.

The goblins looked at one another, but none of them said anything.

Kirsty tried to hide her smile. It was obvious — they *did* want their own book!

"Florence, would you be able to use your magic to make a new memory book for the goblins?" she asked.

"Of course!" Florence said. She smiled at the goblins. "I could make one that would be exactly what you wanted. Maybe the cover could have thorns on it, or slimy patches . . ."

"Oooh!" the goblins cried, their eyes lighting up.

"I'd make the pages green, too," Florence went on. "And I'd even add some special magic so that you can add your favorite smells to the book — IF you give me my book back."

"Favorite *smells*," the knobby-kneed goblin said longingly. "We could put in the smell of moldy toadstools."

"And stinky feet!" another suggested.

All of the goblins looked at one another. "It's a deal!" they chorused.

"Hooray!" cheered Kirsty, Rachel, and Florence. The little fairy got to work right away. She waved her wand and muttered some magic words. Seconds later, a big green book appeared in the tallest goblin's hands. It was oozing with some yucky-smelling slime, and had a sticky, prickly cover.

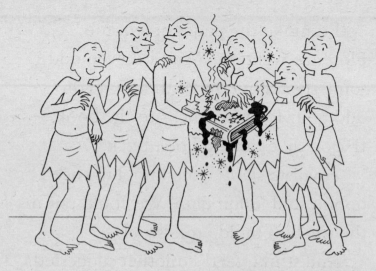

"Oh," said the tallest goblin, stroking the book. "It's so ugly. It's perfect!" He turned to the smallest goblin. "Go ahead, hand over her book," he ordered. "This is worth *fifty* silly fairy memory books!"

The smallest goblin thrust Florence's memory book toward the little fairy. With a smile of delight, she waved her wand, and it shrank to fairy-size in the goblin's hand. Then she fluttered down and picked it up. "Thank you," she said happily.

The goblins wandered off, excitedly discussing what smells they'd add to their new book and how Jack Frost would love their horrid handiwork.

"Take your time," Florence called after them. "Memory books, like true friendships, can't be rushed!" Then she smiled at Kirsty and Rachel. "And now it's time to repair my memory book — and all the others that have been ruined!"

She touched her wand to her memory book. Bright, shimmering waves of magic began to pulse from it, spreading

through the air in sparkling ripples of
light.

"There," she said happily, as the last
light flickered and disappeared.
"Everything should be fixed, and your
memory book will be full
again." She smiled.

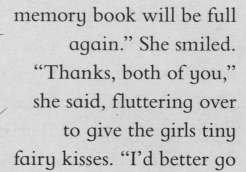

"Thanks, both of you,"
she said, fluttering over
to give the girls tiny
fairy kisses. "I'd better go
back to Fairyland now, to finish getting
everything ready for tomorrow's
Friendship Day. See you soon, I hope!
Oh, and maybe you should take a look
in that shopping bag?"

"In the shopping bag?" Kirsty asked,
glancing down at the empty canvas bag
that still hung from her arm.

"Bye!" Florence called mischievously, vanishing.

Kirsty opened the bag and peeked inside. Then she smiled.

"What is it?" Rachel asked, trying to see.

Kirsty pulled out two pink invitations with their names written in silver ink. *"You are invited to the fairies' Friendship Day at the Fairyland Palace,"* she read, beaming. "Oh, Rachel! How exciting!"

"Hooray!" Rachel cheered, hugging Kirsty happily. She grinned as they began walking toward the stores. "I knew this was going to be another good vacation together, Kirsty. I just knew it!"

The Friendship
Ribbon

Contents

Party Preparations   51

Off to Fairyland!   59

Goblin Games   69

Ribbons for Racing   79

Party Time!   87

Party Preparations

"Good morning, everyone!" Mrs. Tate said to the gathered crowd. "And thank you so much for offering to help out. There's a lot to do!"

It was the next day, and Kirsty and Rachel had come to the village hall with Kirsty's mom and a group of villagers. They were all there to help with preparations for the grand reopening party.

The hall had recently been redecorated, with the whole community's help. It was being renamed the Wetherbury Friendship Hall.

"We have balloons, streamers, and ribbons to sort through and hang up,"

Mrs. Tate said, "music to organize, lights to arrange . . . Oh, and the banner! Kirsty and Rachel, would you help me unroll it, please?" Rachel, Kirsty, and her mom carefully unrolled the large white banner, until everyone could see what was written on

it: WELCOME TO THE WETHERBURY
FRIENDSHIP HALL!

"It doesn't look very exciting at the
moment, but I brought some colorful
paints," Mrs. Tate went on. "And since this
party is all about friendship and working
together, I thought it would be nice if lots
of different people could each paint in a
letter of the banner," she explained.
"That way, it'll look really bright and
eye-catching. OK? Let's get started!"

The team of helpers immediately got to
work — some blowing up balloons,

others untangling the long strings of ribbon and sparkly strands of lights.

"Should we paint our letters on the banner first?" Kirsty asked Rachel.

"Good idea," Rachel said. "Let's take it into one of the side rooms, so it won't get in anyone's way."

The girls carried the banner and paint into a smaller room off the main hall. The room had a piano at one end, and lots of chairs stacked up along the walls. They spread the banner out on the floor, then chose their colors and brushes. Kirsty took the pink paint, while Rachel

decided on purple. Then both girls carefully filled in one letter each.

"This is going to look great when everyone's painted their letters," Rachel said, admiring their work.

"Definitely," said Kirsty with a smile. She was just about to go and wash out her paintbrush when she heard a tiny sigh of relief from behind her.

"There you are!" came a familiar voice. "I'm so glad to see you both. I really need your help again!"

Both girls turned to see Florence the Friendship Fairy flying through an open window, her pretty face looking pale and anxious.

"What happened?" Rachel asked. "Are you OK?"

Florence fluttered down to land on the jar of green paint, her wings drooping. "No, not really," she said sadly. "Today is the fairies' Friendship Day, but everything is going wrong . . . and it's the goblins' fault again! They ran off with my friendship ribbon. If I don't get it back, the party will be a disaster!" She sighed. "Can you come to Fairyland with me and help look for it?"

"Of course!" Kirsty said at once. Then she paused and bit her lip. "The only thing is, we're supposed to be helping my mom here."

"Don't worry," Florence said. "Time will stand still in the human world while you're with me in Fairyland. Is that all right?"

Rachel nodded, her eyes lighting up at the thought of another fairy adventure. "Perfect," she replied.

Florence smiled. "Then let's go — there's no time to lose!"

Off to Fairyland!

Florence waved her wand and a stream
of pink sparkles swirled all around Rachel
and Kirsty, lifting them off the ground
in a glittering whirlwind. The room
became a blur of colors before their eyes!
They felt themselves spinning through
the air, growing smaller and smaller
and smaller. . . .

A few minutes later, their feet touched the ground, and the sparkly whirlwind slowly vanished. Kirsty realized that they were on the grounds of the Fairyland Palace. Lots of fairies she recognized were busily working away. The girls were back in Fairyland — and they were fairies now, too, with their own shimmering wings!

Rachel beamed at Kirsty. Fairyland was the most exciting place ever!

"Look, there's Polly the Party Fun Fairy," she said, pointing as she spotted the little blond fairy across the courtyard. "Oh, and Melodie the Music Fairy, too."

Polly appeared to be working on a new party game that involved teams of fairies competing to fly up and collect glittering gold stars from a nearby tree. Melodie was busy listening to the Music Fairies

rehearse. But both fairies seemed to be having problems!

Florence bit her lip anxiously as Polly's fairies bumped into one another in mid-air and crashed to the ground with surprised shouts. Melodie put her head in her hands at the squeaks and squawks the musicians were making.

"Oh, no." Florence sighed. "Things are still no better here. We have to find my friendship ribbon! Without it, the party is going to be awful."

"What *is* the friendship ribbon?" Kirsty asked, confused.

Florence opened her mouth to reply, but then gave a shout of warning instead. "Phoebe! Watch out!"

Rachel and Kirsty turned to see Phoebe the Fashion Fairy pushing a rack of gorgeous party dresses along a cobbled path nearby. The clothing rack was bouncing on the cobblestones, and some of the dresses and accessories had slipped off their hangers onto the ground without

Phoebe realizing. Phoebe heard Florence's shout and spotted the fallen items. Before she could pick them up, Zoe the Skating Fairy zoomed up behind her carrying a huge box . . . and roller-skated right over the dresses, completely ruining them!

"Oh, no!" Phoebe wailed in dismay. "My dresses!"

Zoe skidded around to see what had happened, and threw up her hands in horror — dropping the box she'd been carrying. It landed with a crash. "Oh, no!" she echoed. "Your dresses — and

the best royal china plates — are
ruined!"

Florence looked like she wanted to cry.
"This is getting worse and worse!" she
said. She turned back to Kirsty and
Rachel. "The friendship ribbon is always
tied to the maypole," she explained,
pointing to where a tall golden pole

stood in the center of the lawn. The three fairies fluttered over to it. "While it's there, it means that friends can work together well, and have fun. It was going to be used in a special friendship dance around the maypole tonight — but the goblins saw the ribbon and decided *they* wanted to play with it. And ever since

they took it down, things have been
going all wrong."

"We'll help you find the ribbon,"
Rachel promised her. "Come on, let's
start looking for it — and those sneaky
goblins, too!"

Goblin
Games

Florence, Kirsty, and Rachel fluttered up
into the air and flew above the palace
grounds, keeping a lookout for any signs
of goblins below. They passed the
bakery, where it smelled as if something
was burning. Then they flew over the
party-decoration workshop.

Grace the Glitter Fairy had just accidentally knocked over a huge barrel of sequins, which poured out in a sparkling flood all over the floor. "Oh, *no*!" they heard her cry in exasperation. Florence had told

them that the friendship ribbon was long, bright blue, and covered in stars. As the three friends flew past the palace stables and across the lake, there was no sign of it — or the goblins — anywhere.

"Let's try looking in here," Florence suggested, pointing to a small wooded area up ahead. Kirsty and Rachel followed their fairy friend as she swooped between the shady trees.

Birds sang sweetly and a light breeze rustled the leaves as the three fairies flew through the woods. Then Florence landed abruptly and turned, putting a  finger to her lips before ducking behind a large tree trunk. Rachel and Kirsty could hear muffled shouts and cheers. They hurried to hide behind trees of their own as they realized that there was a group of goblins gathered in a clearing up ahead. Peering around their trees, they could see that six goblins were playing with the magic ribbon — using it as a sparkly jump rope at first, and then as a rope for tug-of-war.

Florence's eyes were wide with alarm.

"They better not rip my ribbon!" she
murmured. "I can't bear to watch!"

The goblins were split into two teams
of three for the game. Eventually, one
team pulled the others over a branch on
the ground that they were using as a
marker.

"We win!" cried the tallest goblin on
the winning team. He let go of the
ribbon to celebrate with his teammates.

Then he taunted the other team. "Losers! Losers!"

"Your team *cheated*!" argued a frowning goblin on the other team, putting his hands on his hips. "That's not fair. I don't want to be friends with you anymore."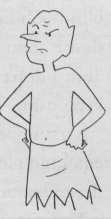

The two goblins started fighting, and another goblin had to break them up. "Hey, stop it! This is supposed to be our Friendship Party," he reminded them. "Anything the fairies can do, we can do better — right?"

"Right," muttered the tall goblin.

"How about a game of blind goblin's buff?" the smallest goblin suggested. "We can use the ribbon as a blindfold."

Florence beckoned Kirsty and Rachel behind a shrub while the goblins began arguing over who was going to be the blind goblin first. "I really need to get that ribbon from them," she whispered, "but I don't know how we can. They keep using it in all their games!"

Kirsty nodded. "They're really enjoying playing with it, aren't they?" she murmured.

The girls watched as the smallest

goblin ended the argument about who
would be blindfolded first by tying the
ribbon quickly around his own head.
The other goblins dodged him, giggling
as he blundered around, arms
outstretched, trying to catch one of them.

But the goblins didn't play nicely for
very long. One of them picked up a stick
and used it to jab the blindfolded goblin
in the ribs.

"Ow!" he yelped, flailing around. The others cracked up laughing.

Then another one of the goblins threw a handful of acorns at the blindfolded one. He cried out in surprise as they *ping*ed off his pointy nose. "Stop it!" he yelled, running toward the noise of the other goblins' cackles. "Stop!"

Rachel, Kirsty, and Florence, meanwhile, were still trying to come up with a plan to get the ribbon. It was hard to think straight, with the noise of the squabbling goblins in the background. Then Kirsty smiled. "I have an idea!" she whispered.

Ribbons for Racing

"Florence, could you use your magic to make some other ribbons that look the same as the friendship ribbon?" Kirsty asked.

Florence nodded. "Of course," she said. "They won't be quite as sparkly as the friendship ribbon, but —"

"That's fine," Kirsty said, interrupting. "In fact, that's perfect! Let's tell the goblins that a three-legged race is the only way to tell who are the best friends. We can use the ribbons to tie up their legs. Hopefully they'll be so distracted by the race that we'll be able to sneak up, take the friendship ribbon, and fly off!"

Florence grinned. "I love it!" she said.

She waved her wand and spoke some magic words under her breath. Then, in a swirl of pink sparkles, two matching ribbons appeared in her hand.

"There!" She smiled. "Now let's put our plan into action."

Rachel, Kirsty, and Florence all fluttered into the clearing, just as the smallest goblin ripped off his blindfold. "I'm not playing this game anymore," he grumbled. "You guys are so mean! You're the worst friends ever!"

"Uh-oh," Rachel said loudly. "Worst friends ever? That's not good. We were just wondering which of you are *best* friends."

The goblins all replied at once, pointing as they talked. "I'm best friends with him, but he likes *him* better than me."

"I don't like him or him or him, but *he's* OK, I guess."

"I'm the best at everything, so I must be the best friend," another boasted.

"Well," Kirsty said over their chatter, "what about having a competition to decide who are the best friends of all? We have some extra ribbons here, so you can have a three-legged race. Get into pairs as quickly as you can!"

Kirsty spoke so firmly that the goblins all scurried to find a partner and tie their legs together.

"The first pair to reach the weeping willow tree wins!" Rachel said. "Ready, set, GO!"

The goblins began hobbling off in pairs, all looking very determined. But as they ran, Kirsty began to doubt that her plan would work. The goblins were actually all really good at running three-legged! Would *any* of them fall over?

"Hmmm," said Florence, as if reading Kirsty's mind. "Maybe I should make things a little trickier for them. . . ." She waved her wand and whispered some more magic words. A stream of sparkles swirled out of her wand tip. Suddenly, lots of stones and acorns rolled in front of the goblins' feet!

"Ooh! Ahh!" wailed the goblins. One by one, they stumbled and fell on top of one another!

They weren't hurt, but the goblins
were soon a big tangle of arms and legs,
all shouting and arguing.

"Quick!" Rachel urged. "Now's our
chance to get the ribbon!"

Party Time!

Florence didn't need to be told twice! She zoomed through the air and untied the sparkliest ribbon from the tangle of goblin legs, then fluttered up high. "Got it!" she cheered. "Come on, let's fly back and tie it to the maypole!"

Rachel and Kirsty soared into the air after Florence, and the three of them flew all the way back to the palace grounds. There, Florence tied the magic ribbon back on the maypole. "Hooray!" they cheered, hugging one another in triumph.

"Is that Kirsty and Rachel I see?" came a booming voice. The girls turned to see the fairy king and queen walking into the courtyard with big smiles on their faces.

Rachel and Kirsty smiled back politely and dipped into curtsies.

King Oberon and Queen Titania were
always really nice, but the girls still felt
shy in front of them. "Hello," they said
together.

Florence flew down from the maypole.
"Kirsty and Rachel have helped me twice
in the last two days, Your Majesties," she
said. "Yesterday
they helped me
get my magic
memory
book from
the goblins,
and today
they helped
rescue the
friendship ribbon. They are true friends
to the fairies!"

Queen Titania smiled and nodded.

"Girls, we would be honored if you two could declare our Friendship Party officially open," she said. She waved her wand, and the sound of a bell ringing majestically echoed through the air. All the fairies fell silent and turned to see what was happening.

Holding hands, Rachel and Kirsty looked at each other and then said, "We declare the fairy Friendship Party officially . . . OPEN!"

A great cheer rose as the celebrations
began. Melodie and her orchestra
played some beautiful music, while
another group of fairies performed a
special friendship dance around the
maypole. Then everyone went into the
Great Hall of the palace for some party
games with Polly. Grace the Glitter
Fairy had decorated the hall with the
most wonderful pink and silver
streamers!

Rachel and Kirsty had a fantastic time! Polly's new party games were a lot of fun. They played Best Friend Hide-and-Seek, joined in some obstacle-course races and a treasure hunt, and then took a Best Friend Fun Quiz. It was wonderful to see so many of their fairy friends again, especially since everyone was enjoying themselves so much!

A little later, Cherry the Cake Fairy and Honey the Candy Fairy made all sorts of delicious food appear. Kirsty and Rachel couldn't wait to try Cherry's delicious rose-and-lavender cupcakes, and Honey's Fairy Fizz Drops and

Magic Marshmallow Melts. "Delicious," Kirsty said, licking her lips. "Thank you, Honey. Those are the yummiest candies I've ever tasted!"

"And the fluffiest cupcakes, too," Rachel said, smiling at Cherry. "What a great Friendship Party this is!"

Just then, King Oberon and Queen Titania appeared beside the girls. "Thanks again for everything you've done for the fairies," the king said. "I'm afraid we need to send you back to your world now, but I hope you'll be back before too long."

Florence flew over to say good-bye.

"Thanks from me, too," she said. "It's wonderful to be friends with you!"

"It's wonderful to be friends with *all* of you," Kirsty replied, her eyes shining.

"See you soon, I hope," Rachel said. The queen pointed her wand at them and spoke a magic command. Golden fairy dust billowed from her wand, spinning around the girls and whisking them away in a glittering whirlwind. Seconds later, they were back in the village hall, next to the banner and paints. But something was different.

"Look, Kirsty!" Rachel whispered in delight. She pointed to the letters they'd painted on the banner, and Kirsty's eyes widened. The pink letter she'd painted was now edged with shiny gold paint, and Rachel's purple letter had been patterned with tiny silver hearts.

"Fairy magic," Kirsty said with a smile. "Don't they look pretty?"

At that moment, Mrs. Tate came into the room. "Nice work, girls," she said, when she saw they'd been painting. Then she took a closer look. "Wow!" she exclaimed. "Those letters are beautiful. You did such a great job!"

Rachel and Kirsty exchanged a secret

smile. They knew they couldn't take all the credit for the painting. Fairy magic had made their letters look extra-special — but the two friends weren't about to tell Mrs. Tate that!

The Friendship Bracelets

Contents

Village Celebrations   103

Florence Flies In!   111

That's Magic!   121

Tricks . . . and Treasure!   131

The Hunt Is On!   143

Village Celebrations

"Hold still! There," said Kirsty Tate, zipping up the dress her best friend, Rachel Walker, was wearing.

"Thanks." Rachel smiled. "I'm really looking forward to this party, Kirsty!"

The two girls were in Kirsty's bedroom, getting ready for a special celebration in Wetherbury, where Kirsty lived.

A year earlier, the Wetherbury Village Hall had closed because it needed a lot of repairs. Since then, a team of volunteers had worked hard to rebuild parts of the hall. They had put on a new roof and redecorated the building from top to bottom. Now, at last, it was finished! It had been renamed the Wetherbury

WETHERBURY FRIENDSHIP HALL

Friendship Hall in honor of the great teamwork that had gone into it. Kirsty's mom had helped organize a big party for the villagers and all their friends that night, to mark the hall's reopening.

Rachel and her family had come to

stay with the Tates for school break, so they were going to the party, too. And, best of all, Rachel and Kirsty were in the middle of another fairy adventure! Florence the Friendship Fairy looked after special friendships in both Fairyland and the human world. But, as usual, mean Jack Frost and his goblins were determined to ruin things!

So far, the girls had helped Florence get her magical memory book and her special friendship ribbon back, after they had been stolen by the goblins. They hoped that all of Florence's magic was safe and sound now.

The party was in full swing when Kirsty, Rachel, and their families arrived at the hall. The girls had helped decorate the main room earlier. It looked wonderful, with pink and red streamers and matching balloons. Rachel and Kirsty knew there

would be lots of games later — a treasure
hunt, a cookout, and even a magician!

"Wow, this is great," Rachel said.

"It is," Kirsty agreed. "But nobody
really seems to be enjoying themselves. I
wonder why?"

Rachel looked closer. To her surprise, she could see angry expressions on some kids' faces! Nearby, two boys glared at each other. "There's no way football is better than baseball," one snarled.

"You don't know what you're talking about!"

Other kids with grumpy faces sat on the chairs lining the room, not speaking to anyone.

Mr. and Mrs. Tate didn't seem to notice, so they took Rachel's parents off to introduce them to some other friends. Kirsty and Rachel hovered at the edge of the party, wondering what was going on. "I have a feeling that something is wrong," Kirsty said.

"It's awful, isn't it?" came a little voice from behind them. "I'm so glad you're here!"

Florence Flies In!

Kirsty and Rachel turned to see a tiny fairy peeking out from behind one of the nearby balloons. It was Florence the Friendship Fairy!

"Hello again, girls," she said. "I'm afraid I need your help one more time." Her shoulders drooped, and she suddenly looked upset. "I think it's all my fault that friends aren't getting along at this party!"

"I'm sure it's not," Kirsty said, feeling sorry for poor Florence. "Why don't we go somewhere quieter, and you can tell us what happened?"

Florence agreed and fluttered under Kirsty's hair so that she would stay hidden. The girls went outside and around to the back of the hall, where nobody could see them.

Florence flitted out from her hiding place and perched on some ivy growing up the wall. "You've helped me so much over the last couple days," she began, "and I know how many times you've helped the other fairies, too. We all really value your friendship."

Rachel felt a happy glow. "We love being friends with you all, too," she said.

Florence smiled. "I'm glad to hear it," she said. "I wanted to give you each a special friendship bracelet as a gift, to say thank you. So after our Friendship Party last night, I asked the Rainbow Fairies to contribute strands of colored thread to the bracelets. When I had the seven colors of the rainbow, I added an extra gold thread that was full of my special friendship magic. Then I wove them all together into two bracelets."

"Ooh, how pretty!" Kirsty exclaimed.

Florence's face fell. "They were pretty," she replied. "I even worked in some extra-special wishing magic that would grant you both a wish when you were wearing the bracelets. But unfortunately, Jack Frost overheard me telling the Rainbow Fairies about my plans. He didn't want you to have the bracelets, so he ordered his goblins to steal them from my workshop."

"How mean!" Rachel said. "Why doesn't he want us to have them?"

"Maybe he wanted to punish you, because you helped me get the memory book and the friendship ribbon back from his goblins," Florence said sadly. "And you know how cold and cruel he is. He doesn't understand friendship, or wanting to do nice things for other people. He doesn't have many friends himself."

"That's true," Kirsty said thoughtfully. Jack Frost had lots of goblins under his command, but you couldn't really call them friends. "So, does Jack Frost have the bracelets now?"

"No," Florence said. "Those goblins are so sneaky, they decided to have some fun before they took the bracelets to Jack Frost. They heard about this party in Wetherbury and didn't want to miss out, so they came along. And that's the problem."

Rachel frowned, not understanding. "What do you mean?"

"Well, the goblins have the friendship bracelets," Florence went on. "But they don't realize that a friendship bracelet should only be worn by the person it was made for. If someone else wears it, my friendship magic works in reverse! Then the wearer, and anyone near the wearer, starts arguing and breaking up their friendships."

"So that's why we saw people arguing earlier," Kirsty said. "By stealing our bracelets and wearing them here, the goblins are causing everyone to fight with their friends!"

"Exactly," Florence replied sadly. "And I have to stop them before they ruin the whole party. Will you help me find the goblins, and get your bracelets back?"

"Of course," Rachel said right away. "Let's start looking!"

The three friends went back into the village hall. People were dancing, and Kirsty and Rachel peered closely at them. Some kids had put on costumes for the occasion. The dance floor was so crowded that it was hard to make out everybody's faces.

Just then, Rachel noticed two boys heading out onto the dance floor, bickering loudly.

They were both in costumes — one was dressed as a pirate, the other as a knight — but there was no mistaking their long noses and pointy ears. They were goblins!

That's Magic!

"There they are!" Rachel whispered, pointing at the goblins as they stomped across the room. They were arguing about who was the best dancer. Both goblins started dancing to prove that they were better, though they still looked very grouchy.

All around the goblins, new arguments began springing up — silly arguments, at that! "Short hair is better than long hair," one girl snapped at another, who had a long braid. "I don't want to be friends with anyone with long hair."

"I don't like your T-shirt — so I don't like you!" one boy muttered to another.

"This is getting worse by the minute!" Florence groaned. "I'm going to try

sprinkling some friendship magic around.
Hopefully it will help patch up these
arguments."

Kirsty and Rachel watched as Florence
flew high up in the air. They saw her
wave her wand,
and then
streams
of pink
stars
swirled
across
the room.

"Sorry,"
the girl with
short hair said to the girl with the braid.
"I don't know what I was talking about.
Your hair is really pretty."

"I didn't mean to be rude about your

T-shirt," the boy said to his friend. "Let's go outside and play, OK?"

"Florence's magic is working!" Kirsty said happily.

"But so is the magic from the bracelets," Rachel said. "Look!"

It was true. As fast as Florence helped friends make up, new arguments started. The two goblins were still bickering, too. As the pirate goblin shoved the knight, the sleeve of his pirate shirt rode up —

and Kirsty noticed a rainbow-colored bracelet on his wrist. A-ha! "There's one of the bracelets," she whispered to Rachel. "But how can we get it back?"

Before Rachel could reply, the band finished their song. The singer made an announcement. "We're going to take a break now, but a very special guest will be entertaining you while we're away. Here's . . . Milo the Magician!"

A big "Ooooh!" of excitement went up as a man in a cape and top hat walked onstage.

Everyone hurried to grab a chair, including the goblins, and sat down to watch the show. Rachel and Kirsty sat near the back of the hall, with Florence hidden under Kirsty's hair.

"There!" Florence said suddenly, pointing. Kirsty and Rachel leaned forward and counted one, two, THREE goblins sitting in the front row. One wore the pirate costume, one the knight outfit, and the third wore a tall wizard's hat and cloak.

"Oh, no," Rachel said. "Three goblins and two bracelets — this could get tricky."

The magician's show began, and the girls watched curiously. He plucked oranges from behind people's ears and pulled a rabbit from his hat. Kirsty and Rachel thought he was great! Unfortunately, the other kids in the audience were grumpy and restless, glaring at one another. The goblins all seemed to enjoy the tricks, though. They clapped enthusiastically throughout the performance.

When Milo's show ended, Mrs. Tate stepped onto the stage. "We're going to start a game of hide-and-seek now, out in the yard," she said. "Follow me, everyone!"

Most people — including the pirate and the knight goblins — hurried after Kirsty's mom. But the goblin with the wizard's hat stayed where he was. "I want more magic!" he said to Milo, who was packing up his equipment.

"Sorry," Milo said. "Show's over —

even for wizards. Why don't you go outside with the others?"

The goblin didn't budge. "I want more magic," he repeated. As he did, the girls spotted a brightly colored stripe on one of his wrists — the second friendship bracelet!

"I have an idea," Kirsty said excitedly. "If the goblin wants a magic show, maybe *we* could give him one. Then we could use some real magic to get the bracelet away from him!"

Florence grinned. "Let's give it a try!" she said.

Tricks . . . and Treasure!

Milo left the hall, but the goblin stayed right where he was, glaring into space. "Perfect," Florence said. "It's time for us to put on our very own show."

Florence waved her wand, and the girls were suddenly wearing magician costumes — capes, hats, and wands!

"Hi," Rachel said, strolling up in front of the goblin. "You like magic, huh? Want to see another show?"

The goblin blinked in surprise. "Where did you come from?" he asked.

Kirsty tapped her nose mysteriously as she walked up to join Rachel. "Magic," she said. "Now let's see . . . what's this egg doing here?"

She reached behind the goblin's pointy right ear and hoped with all her heart that Florence would be able to help her with the trick! Yes — a smooth egg appeared in her palm at just the right

moment. She drew her hand back to
show the goblin what was in it.

"Wow!" Rachel said, trying not to
laugh at the goblin's startled expression.
"Didn't your parents ever teach you to
wash behind your ears?

"Do some more!" the goblin urged.
"More magic!"

Kirsty pulled off her top hat, and
showed the goblin that it was empty.
"Nothing in there, right?" she said. "But

let's see what happens when I say the
magic words . . . *bibble bobble, bibble bobble!*"

The goblin gasped — and so did
Kirsty. As she finished the magic words,
a beautiful white dove flew straight out
of her hat and through
the open window.
"Whoa!"
the goblin
cried.
"You're
even better
than Milo!"
"And now
for another trick," Rachel announced.
"This may look like an ordinary wand,"
she said, tapping it against the goblin's
wizard hat. "But if I throw it up in the
air and catch it, it turns into . . ." She

held her breath and threw the wand up high. There was a sparkle of pink magic dust. Then a string of colorful silk handkerchiefs shot out of the end of the wand — and started to wrap themselves tightly around the goblin!

"Oooh!" the goblin cried. "That was a good one!"

Kirsty and Rachel watched as the handkerchiefs wound around and around the goblin. Soon he couldn't clap anymore, since his arms were bound tight against his body. The excited light vanished from his eyes. "Hey!" he said. "What's happening?"

"This!" replied Kirsty, as she quickly untied the friendship bracelet from his wrist. "Thank you very much!"

The goblin's mouth fell open as he realized that he'd been tricked. "You — you —" he stuttered. "You horrible magicians! That's not fair!"

"I didn't think it was very fair when you and your friends stole my bracelets, either," Florence said, flying down and landing on Rachel's shoulder.

The goblin made a furious growling noise and stumbled away. "I'll make sure you don't get the other bracelet," he called. "So there!"

Kirsty and Rachel admired the friendship bracelet in Kirsty's hand. It had KIRSTY stitched across it in tiny gold letters. "Here, let me put it on for you," Florence said with a smile. She waved her wand, so that both magician costumes vanished — and the bracelet tied itself neatly around Kirsty's wrist. "Ta-da!"

"It's beautiful," Kirsty said happily.
"Thank you so much, Florence. Now

we just need to
get Rachel's
bracelet back."
"Let's go
see what those
other goblins
are up to,"
Florence said.
She hid in the front
pocket of Rachel's bag, and the girls
headed outside.

As they walked out the front doors,
they almost ran right into the goblins!
The wizard goblin had been untied, and
they all looked very smug. "Looking for
the bracelet, are you?" the knight goblin
said. "Ha! You'll never find it now."

"Yeah," the pirate goblin gloated, showing them his bare wrists. "We've hidden it somewhere really good."

"Listen up, everyone!" Kirsty's mom called just then. "While the grown-ups get the grill started, there's going to be a treasure hunt. There's real treasure at the end, in an actual treasure chest!"

The goblins looked at one another in horror. "What . . . what does the treasure chest look like?" the pirate goblin croaked after a moment.

"It's a small gold box," Mrs. Tate
replied.

The goblins all looked completely
dismayed about something. Rachel
elbowed Kirsty. "I bet they hid the
bracelet in the treasure chest!" she

guessed. "That's why they look so worried!"

"I think you're right," Kirsty said excitedly. "So we have to find the treasure chest before they do!"

The Hunt Is On!

"Here's the first clue," Mrs. Tate told the group. *"Use two sticks to tap on my top, I make a bang — but I'm quiet if you stop!"*

Kirsty solved the clue very quickly. "Two sticks to tap on my top . . . It's a drum," she whispered to Rachel. "It must be the drum that the band used. Come on!"

Kirsty and Rachel began running toward the hall.

"We have to get to the treasure chest first, so we can take the bracelet out before anyone else sees it," Rachel said, panting as they ran. "But how are we going to do that?"

"By flying, of course," Florence said, popping her head out of Rachel's bag. "Find somewhere quiet, and I'll turn you both into fairies!"

Kirsty veered away from the stage and ducked into the bathroom, with Rachel close behind. Florence waved her wand, sending more of her glittering fairy dust spinning all around them. Seconds later, they were fairies! The girls fluttered their wings and flew back into the hall just in time to hear a boy reading the second clue aloud.

"*We're bright and colorful, and filled with air. Tied to a string, the next clue is there. . . .*" he said, frowning.

"Bright and colorful? Sounds like flowers," one girl said eagerly.

Kirsty, Rachel, and Florence, who were perched on one of the ceiling beams, exchanged smiles. "Balloons!" they all said together. "Quick, let's go!"

They soared out into the yard. There was a big bunch of balloons tied to a tree, and they swooped down to land in the middle of them. The third clue was attached to the string of one of the balloons! This clue led them to the front door of the hall. There, they spotted a

large metal mailbox attached to the inside of the door — and what was that, poking out of it?

"It's the treasure chest!" Rachel cheered in excitement.

Kirsty opened the mailbox flap, then opened the gold chest. Sure enough, lying on top of a pile of chocolate coins, was a second friendship bracelet! This one had RACHEL embroidered on it.

"It's beautiful," Rachel exclaimed, taking the bracelet out. "Thank you, Florence!"

"My pleasure," Florence replied, waving her wand and returning the girls to human-size. The bracelet magically tied itself around Rachel's wrist.

Suddenly, they heard footsteps approaching. "Sounds like everyone else is on their way — quick, out the front door!" Florence urged.

Kirsty closed the treasure chest. She
and Rachel ran in a loop around the
building and back through the hall,
with Florence hiding
in Rachel's bag.
They couldn't let
anyone know
that they'd found
the treasure first!
They reached the
front porch again just in
time to hear cheers from the other
kids, who were gathered by the front
door. "Chocolate coins!" someone
whooped. "Yum!"

Rachel had assumed that since she'd
gotten her bracelet, everyone would go
back to being friends, but that wasn't
the case.

The kids by the door — and the goblins! — were pushing and shoving one another in order to snatch up chocolate coins, even though there were plenty to go around.

"Do you remember how I said that I added some special wishing magic to your bracelets when I made them?" Florence said quietly. "Well, now you can make your wish."

Kirsty's eyes lit up with excitement. Rachel's did, too. What should they wish for?

"Since these are friendship bracelets, maybe we should make a friendship wish?" Rachel said after a moment.

"Yes, for everyone here," Kirsty suggested.

Florence beamed. "I couldn't have said it better myself," she said.

Kirsty and Rachel held hands. "We wish that everyone could be friends again!" they said together.

Both girls felt their wrists tingle as sparkly magic flew up into the air. And then . . .

"Sorry I wasn't very nice to you earlier," one boy said to another. "It's cool that we like different sports — it doesn't mean we can't be friends."

"I like pink *and* purple," one girl said to the girl next to her. "But I like being friends with you much more than any color!"

"That's more like it," Florence said happily.

Just then, one of the adults shouted that the cookout was ready, and the kids all ran outside, laughing and joking. Only the goblins stayed behind — and they didn't look happy.

"Cheer up," Florence told them. "Here, let me make you your own friendship bracelets." She waved her wand and three bracelets appeared on the goblins' wrists. They weren't quite as magical-looking as Rachel's and Kirsty's bracelets, but the goblins looked very excited.

"And here's one to take home to Jack
Frost, too," Florence said, creating a
silver bracelet and handing it to the
nearest goblin. "Hopefully this will help
him become a good friend to others.
Maybe even to the fairies!"

The goblins thanked her politely and
went off, all being extra-nice to one
another. "You're the ugliest goblin I've
ever seen," the pirate goblin said sweetly
to the wizard goblin.

"Oh, thank
you!" the
wizard goblin
replied,
blushing. "But
you definitely
have the
pointiest nose!"

Rachel and Kirsty tried their hardest not to burst out laughing. They'd never seen the goblins being so friendly — even if their compliments were strange!

"It's been so nice to meet you," Florence said. "Thank you for all your help! I'd better return to Fairyland now. I'm sure the rest of your party will be lots of fun, now that everyone is friends again."

"Thanks, Florence," Kirsty said. "I love my bracelet — and I love being friends with the fairies!"

"Me, too," Rachel said. "See you soon, I hope."

Florence blew them a kiss and fluttered away. Once she'd gone, Kirsty and Rachel rejoined the party. Everyone was in a great mood, and there was lots of laughter and happy conversation.

"Hooray for friends," Kirsty said, slipping her arm through Rachel's.

Kirsty smiled. "And hooray for fairies, too!" she said. "I hope we have lots more adventures together!"

Don't miss any of Rachel and Kirsty's
other fairy adventures!

Check out this magical
sneak peek of

Lindsay
the Luck Fairy!

Trip to Toberton

"I'm so glad you could come with us," Rachel Walker said to her best friend, Kirsty Tate. "I always have more fun when we're together."

"Me, too," Kirsty said. She grabbed Rachel's hand in the backseat of the car and smiled. The girls always shared such amazing adventures!

This time, they were headed to Toberton, a small village several hours from Rachel's house. Mrs. Walker was going to a convention in the Toberton Hotel over the weekend for work, and everyone else was coming along to enjoy the country air.

"You'll find a lot to do around Toberton, girls," Mrs. Walker said from the front seat. "When I was little, I stayed in a cottage there with my family. It's beautiful."

"That's not what you said when you first read the invitation to the convention. You said Toberton was spooky!" Mr. Walker said with a laugh.

"That's not exactly true," Mrs. Walker corrected him, smiling. She turned and looked into the backseat. "My brothers, who were much older, told me the woods were haunted with fairies, goblins, and leprechauns. I was so young that I believed them. I even imagined seeing green shadows hiding in the trees. It's silly, I know."

Rachel and Kirsty didn't think it sounded silly at all! The two girls *knew* that fairies and other magical creatures were real. In fact, they were friends with the fairies! The girls had assisted the fairies on many occasions. Whenever Jack Frost and his naughty goblins had evil plans, the king and queen of Fairyland asked Rachel and Kirsty for help.

"While Mom is in her meetings, we can explore the town and the nearby landmarks," Mr. Walker said from the driver's seat. "I'll bet there are some great wildflowers in the woods, too."

Kirsty and Rachel smiled at each other. Mr. Walker really liked flowers and wildlife.

"Don't forget that I have tomorrow afternoon off," Mrs. Walker added. "And if everything goes as planned with my speech, I can join you for the festival on Sunday."

Today was only Friday, but Sunday was St. Patrick's Day, and there would be a festival in the center of town to celebrate. The girls couldn't wait!

"It sounds like we'll be busy," Kirsty said, grinning with excitement.

"How long until we get there?" Rachel asked.

"Well, we would be there already, if
we hadn't had to turn around," said Mrs.
Walker.

"Don't worry, dear. We should still
make it on time," Mr. Walker said.

Rachel bit her lip. Her mom had lost
her glasses, and they'd had to go back
home to get her other pair. Then they
had run into a lot of traffic. Now they
were really running late. What bad luck!

As soon as they pulled into the
hotel's circular driveway, Mrs. Walker
jumped out of the car and rushed inside.
Mr. Walker opened the trunk and
handed each girl her own duffel bag.
Then he grabbed the bag that he and
Mrs. Walker shared. As he slammed the
trunk closed, Rachel thought she saw
something flash by in a shimmery glow.

"Did you see that?" Rachel whispered to Kirsty.

Kirsty looked around and shook her head. "No," she answered.

Rachel frowned. "It was probably nothing."

RAINBOW magic

These activities are magical!
Play dress-up, send friendship notes, and much more!

RAINBOW magic™

There's Magic in Every Series!

The Rainbow Fairies
The Weather Fairies
The Jewel Fairies
The Pet Fairies
The Fun Day Fairies
The Petal Fairies
The Dance Fairies
The Music Fairies
The Sports Fairies
The Party Fairies
The Ocean Fairies
The Night Fairies
The Magical Animal Fairies
The Princess Fairies

Read them all!

■■SCHOLASTIC

www.scholastic.com
www.rainbowmagiconline.com

HIT entertainment

RMFAIRY6